For Suzan Lake who taught me how,
and for Daniel who believed I could.
- B.B.

For my sister, who is extraordinary.
- M.E.B.

Extraordinary

written by
Bethany Boster

illustrated by
Megan Elizabeth Baratta

Recess began at Miss Jane's school for girls:
The balls were all bouncing, the merry-go-round whirled,

The jump ropes slapped happily down on the ground,
The sun was all shine, and the birds were all sound.

When suddenly, out came a girl who was new.
The balls stopped their bouncing. The jump ropes stopped too.

The girl had a ponytail, t-shirt, and jeans.
She had a big smile. Her backpack was green.
No one there knew her. Just who could she be?

“I’m Emily,” she said.
“I’m extraordinary.”

The girls introduced themselves. Each said her name,
And hoped that this new girl would kindly explain.

She looked very normal, so what could it be
That made this new classmate extraordinary?

"What makes you so special?"
Asked one girl named Elle.
"Just looking at you it's not easy to tell."

"I guess I just am," is what Emily said.
"I don't have a tail and I don't have three heads,
But I'm as amazing as one girl can be.
There's nobody out there exactly like me."

Then Jillian laughed, and she said with a sneer,
"I'm sorry but boring is what you are, dear.

Just look at me:

dazzling,

snazzy,

unique,

My hair is bright blue, and there's paint on my chee
I wear stripes and plaids with my zebra print socks
My shoes light up red, pink, and blue when I walk

Then Emily smiled and said, “It is true,”
Your clothes are fantastic! Your hair is bright blue!
You’re crazy and wild! You’re one in a million,
But then so am I,” said our hero to Jillian.

MahKQuennaah spoke next and said, “Let me explain,
You cannot stand out with that kind of name.

Try adding two ‘E’s, an ‘H’, and a ‘Y’.
A five that is silent could make you fly high.

Yes, Ehm5iylee’s a name that could take a girl soar
Your parents predestined you to be quite boring.”

"I think there may be a few who'd disagree:
Dickinson, Pankhurst, and Brontë make three -
And I'll be the fourth," said Emily with pride.
"Extraordinary's something that comes from inside."

“Hey, you!” came a call from a young girl named Joy,
“To stand out these days you must act like a boy,
So get into sports, collect bugs, and be tough.
You’ll have to give up all of your girly stuff.
If you must be a princess, then fight with a sword.
Do Kung-fu and Judo or people get bored.”

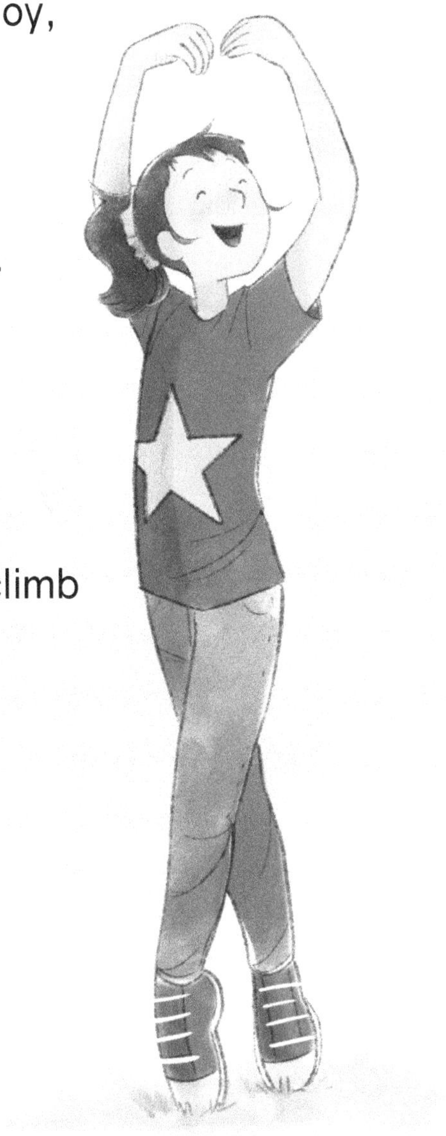

“You run, and catch bugs,” exclaimed Em, “and you climb
That’s awesome! It’s just not how I spend my time.
I like to draw fairies, and I like ballet,
And girly or not, it’s how I like to play.”

"You only do art and ballet and that's all?!
You can't think that's special. Girl, get on the ball!
I'm Ann. I make films. I speak Spanish and Greek.
I practice my cello 10 hours each week.

I'm soccer team captain. I bake fancy cakes.
If awesome's your goal, well then *that's* what it takes."

"You have me impressed," enthused Em with a grin.
"Just hearing your schedule makes my head spin,
But you don't become special by things that you do,
The best kind of special is just being you."

Next Madison spoke saying, “Aren’t you funny,
You *must* know that being important takes money.
When lacking in moolah, dinero, or dough,
The best you can be is just sort of so-so.
Cash improves everything; just look at me.
It’s money that makes you the best you can be.”

“Money does lots of great things, it is true.
But money can’t make you be more or less you,”
Said Em. “What’s inside cannot come from a store,
You’re you when you’re rich, and you’re you when you’re poor.”

Then Margaret stepped up. She was dressed in all black:
Black fingernails, boots, and a black leather hat.
She looked at the group through her bored, black-rimmed eyes,
And said, "Life's a mess, so it's pointless to try.
Unless you're naive, you know life's bleak and dark.
All people are minnows and life is a shark."

Em said, "It is clear you prefer pessimism,
For me, life looks best through a rose-colored prism,
And seeing the good makes me happy, not weak.
I like having sunshine, so that's what I seek."

Then Violet spoke up, saying, “I think I see,
How each of us girls is extraordinary:

I sing in the choir,

and make things with clay,

And I paint the sets when we put on a play,
And each of those things are just small parts of me.
It's being *myself* that's extraordinary."

Emily gave Violet a super high-five,
"You've got it!" she said. "It's important to strive
To be the best you you can possibly be,
But just being you is extraordinary."

And starting that day,
Things were never the same,
For the girls who attended
The school of Miss Jane.

Bethany Boster lives in Utah with her husband Daniel, five children, a handsome dog named Percy, two cats, and a handful of chickens. She is a homeschool mom who loves herbal tea, ballroom dancing, great books, and old movies. To learn more about Bethany's love affair with the English language, join her at thesunnyscribbler.com or on Instagram *@the_sunny_scribbler*.

Megan Elizabeth Baratta is a children's book illustrator livin in upstate New York with her husband Jeremy, and kitten Pip. She loves rendering scenes of ordinary life and showing thei quiet beauty. When she's not at her drawing board, she loves cooking, reading, and sipping coffee.

www.barattastudio.com
@megan.elizabeth.baratta

CPSIA information can be obtained
at www.ICGtesting.com
Printed in the USA
LVHW071113311221
707491LV00002B/9